LOVE AND
FEAR

LOVE AND FEAR

REED FARREL COLEMAN

RAVEN BOOKS
an imprint of
ORCA BOOK PUBLISHERS

Library and Archives Canada Cataloguing in Publication

Coleman, Reed Farrel, 1956–, author
Love and fear / Reed Farrel Coleman.
(Rapid Reads)

Issued in print and electronic formats.
ISBN 978-1-4598-0677-1 (paperback).—ISBN 978-1-4598-0678-8 (pdf).—
ISBN 978-1-4598-0679-5 (epub)

I. Title. II. Series: Rapid reads
PS3553.O47443L69 2016   C813'.54   C2015-904480-4
                  C2015-904481-2

First published in the United States, 2016
Library of Congress Control Number: 2015946326

Summary: PI Gulliver Dowd is pulled into a search for
the missing daughter of the most powerful Mafia don in
New York in this work of crime fiction. (RL 2.7)

*Orca Book Publishers is dedicated to preserving the environment and has
printed this book on Forest Stewardship Council® certified paper.*

Orca Book Publishers gratefully acknowledges the support for
its publishing programs provided by the following agencies:
the Government of Canada through the Canada Book Fund and the
Canada Council for the Arts, and the Province of British Columbia
through the BC Arts Council and the Book Publishing Tax Credit.

Cover design by Jenn Playford
Cover photography by Peter Rozovsky

ORCA BOOK PUBLISHERS
www.orcabook.com

Printed and bound in Canada.

19 18 17 16 • 4 3 2 1

For Jim Bogart and Carrie Robb

ONE

Gulliver Dowd had been this close to finding out why his sister was murdered. This close to finding out who had done it. He had held the envelope with the answers in his misshapen hands. He had also been the one to set the envelope on fire. For most of the last eight years, the answers to these two questions had been his reason for living. Keisha's murder had haunted him. Driven him. Helped turn him into the man he was. Now he had to forget. He had to leave Keisha's murder behind him. Why?

Why does any man turn his back on the past? Love and fear.

He had been forced to choose between the two women who had meant the most to him. The two women who had lifted him out of his bitter life. His life of pain and self-hatred. His sad and lonely life. One of those women—his sister Keisha— was already gone. And gone was gone forever. He could get the answers about her murder, or he could keep Mia safe. That was his choice. Those were his only options. There was no middle ground. And the man who had given Gulliver the choice was a serious man. A dangerous man with even more dangerous friends. The math was cruel but easy to do.

Gulliver's parents had adopted Keisha, just as they had adopted him. Like Gulliver, Keisha was a runt of the litter. But in many ways she was his opposite. Gulliver was pale. A dwarf. A little person. A freak.

It never mattered to him what label you used. He was never going to grow taller. His legs were never going to be the same length. His body was never going to be normal. As much as he hated his smallness, he hated his good looks even more. God's little joke was how Gulliver thought of his handsome face.

Keisha was black, her skin very dark. Always a little heavy. Plain to look at. An abused foster child. But she had overcome all the things the world had put in her way. She had taken all the pain in her life and turned it into love. She had gotten herself into shape. Gone to college. Made it through the police academy at the top of her class. All that only to be murdered, her body left behind a vacant building in East New York.

In a very real way, it was Keisha's death that had given Gulliver life. Until his sister's murder, he hadn't really lived. A day was something to suffer through, not something to enjoy. He had only one friend—Rabbi. He'd had only one girlfriend—Nina—and then only for a few months in high school. But the need to solve Keisha's murder had changed him. It had given him a reason to live. Her death had led him to study martial arts. To learn how to shoot. To earn his private investigator's license. As true as all that was, as much as he loved his sister and wanted justice for her, what did it matter? Keisha was like Humpty Dumpty. The answers were like all the king's horses and all the king's men. All the answers in the world wouldn't bring Keisha back again.

Gulliver had to choose Mia. Mia was alive. Mia was his present and his future. And Gulliver knew it would only take a single whisper from one powerful man to another to end Mia's life. Gulliver's was the choice everyone in his shoes would have made. Rabbi had told him as much.

Rabbi who had grown up with Gulliver and Keisha. Rabbi who loved Keisha like a second big sister. So too had Ahmed. Ahmed who had gone to school with Keisha. Ahmed who had dated Keisha before he went into the Navy. But the choice ate at Gulliver. It tore at him.

He felt tortured every time he looked at Mia. Every time he kissed her or held her in his arms. He felt tortured because he had turned his back on Keisha. He felt tortured because he could not stand the thought of losing Mia. But that was just what had happened.

His guilt and fear had made him push Mia away. They were no longer living together. She had stayed in their condo in Brighton Beach. He had moved back into his office in Red Hook. Mia didn't understand why Gulliver had changed. Why he seemed so far away. Why he seemed so cold to her. And he could not explain it.

How could he tell her she was in danger again? How could he make sense of it to her? No, Mia was better off without him. She was safer without him.

Gulliver opened his eyes. Yawned. Smiled. Reached over to the other side of the bed for Mia. But this wasn't their bed. It wasn't a bed at all. And Mia wasn't there. Old habits die hard. The smile ran away from Gulliver's face as he swung his legs off the couch. Not even the bright sunlight pouring into the office could bring his smile back. He laughed a sad laugh at himself, for he had ended up where he began. His office was once Keisha's loft. He had moved into the loft after she was killed, in order to feel closer to her.

For years it had been his office and his home. Now there was much less space than there used to be. When he'd moved to Brighton Beach with Mia, he had built walls around his office and rented the rest of the loft space to a group of artists. That was okay. Small spaces suited him. And so too did building walls around things. Walls around his office. Walls around his heart.

With the smell of freshly brewed coffee thick in the air, Gulliver sat at his desk. He had showered and dressed. He didn't bother shaving. What for? Who for? As he sat there, he could feel himself slipping back into his old bitter self. When he was working cases, it was easier to forget. It was easier to forget about the choice he had made. Easier to forget about missing Mia. Easier to forget about who he really was and what he really looked like. But he was between cases, and the mirror had stopped lying to him. All he saw when he looked into it was the little, lonely freak he had always been.

He couldn't know that the knock at his door would change everything forever.

TWO

Gulliver Dowd was shocked to see the man standing in the doorway, but he acted like he didn't care. He didn't like this man very much. That was fair enough, because the man liked Gulliver even less than Gulliver liked him. But they had a kind of respect for each other. The kind of respect an enemy has for his toughest foe.

"Good morning, Tony," Gulliver said.

"Morning to you, Bug," said Tony.

Tony was a tough guy. Thick-necked. Barrel-chested. Good with his fists. And mean. He carried a 9mm Beretta in a shoulder holster. Gulliver knew this because he had once taken it away from him. He had disarmed Tony and beaten him up in front of his boss. Gulliver had to do things like that all the time because of his size and misshapen body. People never took him seriously. They turned away. They whispered. They laughed. Gulliver hated the laughing. But he hated most of all people pitying him. So he always had to battle to prove his worth to people. To prove that he too could be a dangerous man. A man to be taken seriously.

Gulliver was unhappy to see Tony because the big man was a living, breathing reminder of the one person Gulliver never wanted to think about again. That person was Tony's boss, Joey "Dollar Menu" Vespucci.

Joey Vespucci was the only Mafia don who'd been left standing after the Justice Department wiped out most of the old New York City mob. And it was Joey Vespucci who had made Gulliver choose between Keisha and Mia. He was the man who had handed Gulliver the envelope with the answers to Keisha's murder. He was the man who would have threatened Mia if Gulliver had chosen to see what was in the envelope. Joey Vespucci was the man who'd given Gulliver the lighter with which to set the envelope on fire.

"Come on in. You want coffee? I just made some," Gulliver said, then turned and hobbled back into the office.

"Sure, Bug." Tony always called him Bug. "Milk and sugar."

Gulliver spun around on his heel. "This is my turf, Tony. My office. In here, you call me Gulliver or Dowd or Sir."

Tony puffed out his chest. He looked like he was going to give Gulliver a hard time. But instead he gave in. "Okay, Dowd. You're right. On your turf you deserve respect."

Gulliver shook his head at the big man.

"What is it, Bug—I mean, Dowd?" Tony asked. "Didn't I just say a man deserves respect on his own turf?"

"People deserve respect period, Tony. All people. They shouldn't have to earn it or be on their own turf to get it."

"That ain't how my world operates."

Gulliver nodded. "I know." He handed Tony his coffee.

"Good stuff, Dowd. Thanks."

Gulliver sipped his coffee and waited for Tony to get to the point. Gulliver was in no rush. He had finished his most recent case a few days ago and had nothing to do. That was the worst thing for Gulliver these days. When he was busy he could focus on the job at hand. It didn't matter whether it was finding a runaway kid or a runaway dog. The important thing was keeping himself busy. Keeping his mind busy. When he wasn't busy, all he could think about was how much he missed Mia.

Tony looked around the office. His eyes landed on the couch, on the blankets and pillows. It was obvious it had been slept on. "You and that girlfriend of yours split up or something?" he said.

Gulliver got a sick look on his face, like he'd been kicked in the stomach. That was answer enough for Tony. He was a tough guy but not a stupid one.

"That's too bad, Dowd. She was pretty, and she seemed to really love you." Tony shook his head and smiled.

"What?" Gulliver asked.

"Not for nothing, Dowd, but how do you do it? No disrespect or nothing—you got a nice face and all, but the rest of you ain't much to look at."

"That's not disrespecting me. It's telling the truth. I'm short and disfigured. But I'm not blind. I see who looks back at me from the mirror."

"And still you land women like that Mia and Nina. Nina was smoking hot. How do you do it?"

Gulliver thought of many answers to that question. One even made him laugh. But what he said was, "You know how women love wounded animals and strays? It's like that. Women love wounded men too. It appeals to their mothering natures. And you don't even have to look at me twice to see I got all kinds of wounds. Inside and out."

Tony lifted his coffee cup to salute Gulliver. "You ain't gonna hear no argument from me on that."

Gulliver lifted his cup too. He smiled.

He let some time pass, then said, "Okay, Tony. This has been nice. We've spoken to each other for a few minutes without throwing a punch or pulling our weapons. We haven't insulted each other too bad, and we've shared a cup of coffee. Now how about telling me why you're here."

Tony's face flushed. His mouth opened and closed a few times. The words seemed not to want to come out. He just couldn't seem to say what he wanted to say. Gulliver helped him.

"Come on, Tony. You came this far. It must be pretty important for you to swallow your pride and come see me this way. Just say it."

"It's the boss," Tony said. His voice was strained.

"Joey Vespucci?"

Tony nodded.

"What about him?" Gulliver asked.

Again Tony hesitated.

"Tony, come on already. Don't make this like pulling teeth. Just say it."

"The boss needs your help."

"Fuck him!" Gulliver said.

"You owe him. He helped you before. I know he did. For what Nina did to him, she should've gotten whacked. You know it and I know it, but he let her walk away because he likes you. He respects you. And I know he helped you with that thing last year. You know, when your cop buddy got killed on the boardwalk in Coney Island."

Gulliver clenched his fists. "I owe him nothing."

"I think you do."

"Did he send you?"

Tony shook his head. "No way. He's got too much pride for that. He'd probably kill me with his own hands if he knew I was here asking for your help."

"Sorry, Tony. If it was for you, I might help. But Joey…nope. Not after what he did to me."

Tony looked panicked. "But it ain't really about the boss."

Gulliver looked at his watch. "I'm listening. Tick...tick...tick."

"It's about his youngest daughter, Bella."

"What about her?"

"She's gone."

"Gone?"

"Gone," Tony repeated.

"How do you mean? Did she run away? Was she abducted? What?"

"I don't think she was abducted," Tony said. "It would take a big set of stones to kidnap Joey Vespucci's kid."

Gulliver plopped himself down in his desk chair. He rubbed his unshaven cheeks. He remembered his trips to Vespucci's mansion in the Todt Hill area of Staten Island. He remembered Joey proudly showing him the photos of his daughters on the mantelpiece. He pictured their faces. They were all pretty. Though Joey had never named them, Gulliver thought he knew which one was the youngest. He recalled that she had a full, pleasant face. Sparkling green eyes and dark brown hair. A distant stare. There was a beautiful sadness about her. Sadness was something Gulliver Dowd knew about no matter how it showed itself. Bella's older sisters were prettier by most standards but with less depth.

He thought on Tony's request for a long time. It wasn't Bella's fault she was Joey Vespucci's daughter. Her father's sins weren't hers to bear or pay for. She hadn't been part of Keisha's murder. She hadn't given Gulliver the impossible choice. Still, he could not bring himself to do this for Vespucci. After all Gulliver had done to dig himself out of his misery, the man had ruined his life.

"No," Gulliver finally said. "I can't do it, Tony. Like I said, if it was for anybody else, I would do it in a second. But after what your boss did to me, I can't. I can recommend—"

Before Gulliver could finish, Tony had put his head into his hands and started sobbing. Sobbing loudly. His thick body shaking.

"Then do it for me, Dowd," he said through his tears.

"Why? Look, I know you must be close to Joey's kids, but—"

"She ain't his, Dowd." Tony thumped his chest. "Bella is mine! She's mine."

THREE

Gulliver couldn't quite believe the words that had just come out of his enemy's mouth. Remembering the faces of the women in the photos on Joey Vespucci's mantel, Gulliver realized that all of them looked at least a little bit like their mother, Maria. He could do simple math too.

"Holy shit!" Gulliver said without meaning to.

"That's right, Dowd. Joey would have me cut up into little pieces and fed to the pigs on his friend's farm in Jersey if he knew.

Now you know. That's three people in the world who do—Maria, me and you."

"How?"

"How do you think? Me and Maria, we slept together and made a beautiful baby."

"I figured that part out. I mean, how did you and Maria get together in the first place?"

Tony looked as if he had just swallowed a handful of broken glass. Gulliver guessed this was something Tony had hardly discussed even with Maria. By talking about it here, Tony was handing Gulliver a dangerous weapon. Something Gulliver could hold over the big man's head forever.

"I'll do it." The words came out of Gulliver's mouth as if by themselves. "I'll take the case, but first I need to know everything."

Tony gave Gulliver a look full of mixed feelings. Joy. Relief. Worry. Panic. Pain. Love. It was a look of a thousand things.

"Joey's older than me, but we been kicking around together since we was kids in Gravesend. Both of our dads were, you know, in the business. Fact is, my dad was higher up the food chain than Joey's dad was, but I was always better with my hands than my head. I never wanted to be nobody's boss. I like being strong, but power don't interest me much."

"This is interesting, Tony, but…"

"Anyways, Joey always got the girls. Always. He's such a handsome guy, and he can talk. Man, can he talk. Always could. My mom used to say Joey could charm a snake without a flute. But when we was in high school, Maria and I was always circling each other. You know how it is. I liked her. She liked me. And we even got together once. I was her first." Tony beamed with pride. "But then Joey noticed her when she got all pretty, and that was that. Joey, he always gets what he wants."

Gulliver nodded. "Yeah, I can see that."

"I could live with him and Maria being together. All I ever wanted was for Maria to be happy. And if Joey made her happy, then I would eat it and be glad for them. Thing is, Maria was never enough for Joey. Even when we was kids and he took her away from me, he had other girls all the time. But that wasn't my business no more. Maria made her choice, and it wasn't me. After a few years, Joey had worked his way up, and he brung me with him. I been by his side ever since."

As Tony spoke, he seemed hurt and angry. He kept clenching and unclenching his fists. His top lip twitched. His eyes turned mean and cold. Ice cold. Gulliver guessed these were things Tony had kept inside a long time. And only when he said them did he feel how deeply he was hurt by them and how mad they made him.

"Didn't it kill you to be so close to Maria all the time?"

He shook his head—hard. Almost like he was telling himself not to answer. "I guess I always hoped she would come back to me or..." He didn't finish the sentence.

"Or if something violent happened to Joey, you would be there waiting for her."

"Something like that."

"Okay, Tony, I get that much. You went along with it for a lot of years. Then you stopped going along with it. What changed?"

"Like I said, Joey always had other women. But he also never got crazy with it. Never did stuff to risk his marriage or hurt his little girls. Then Joey got real involved with a model he met at one of his clubs in the city. Her name was Azraella Parks. She was barely twenty years old. Maybe twenty years younger than Joey. She was cute, I guess, if you like women that weigh less than one of my legs. But she got to Joey bad. Real bad. He couldn't get enough of her, and I was always covering for him with Maria best as I could."

Gulliver said, "But Maria knew."

Tony nodded.

"And that's when the affair started between you and Maria?" Gulliver asked.

"Yep. It was hot and heavy for a while there. I mean, Joey was never around or nothing. And me and Maria had lots of years of catching up to do."

"What happened?"

"After a few months Azraella kicked Joey's ass to the curb for that actor. Devon Jenner. You ever hear of him? He has that sitcom about the nasty crippled guy with the two cute nurses who live with him."

"Sure. The guy who got hurt in a skiing accident and never walked without a cane again, right?"

Tony laughed. "That was no skiing accident, Dowd. That was me. Joey wanted me to kill him, but I wouldn't do it. I told Joey it would be too easy to trace back to him. Then, the week after I broke the prick's legs, Maria found out she was pregnant. You can figure out the rest from there. And for eighteen years now, Bella has been our secret. Making her is the one good thing I done in my whole life. I can't lose her."

"Does Maria know you came to me?"

"Yeah. I told her how good you was at this sort of thing, and she gave me her blessing and her help."

"Does Joey know?"

Tony said no. And that Joey had used all of his contacts and pull, but no one could find Bella.

Then Tony laughed. It was a sad laugh. "He even hired some ex-cop private eyes to help find her. But they ain't found shit."

An hour later, Tony walked out of Gulliver's office. He was just as full of mixed feelings as when he arrived. But they were now somewhat different mixed feelings.

For one thing, he had just handed Gulliver Dowd his life on a silver platter. Maria's life too, for that matter. He had risked it all, telling the little man about their affair and about Bella. He had no way of knowing if Gulliver would keep his secret. It wasn't like they were buddies. Beyond that, he was not at all comfortable with the fee the private eye had demanded. Gulliver had refused the large sum that Tony offered him to find his girl. What Gulliver wanted in return for finding Tony's secret daughter was just as dangerous as any affair Tony had had. Just as dangerous as anything he'd ever done. Gulliver wanted answers. Not just any answers. Gulliver wanted the answers that were in the envelope he'd been forced to burn to save his girlfriend's life.

FOUR

Gulliver was good at finding missing things. It was a talent he was born with. He liked to think it was because he was built low to the ground, like a hound. There was some truth in that. He saw the world from a lower vantage point. Not from six feet up. Not even from five feet up. At just over four feet, he had a grown man's head, a teenager's wounded heart and a child's view of the world. Most adults didn't understand how that made Gulliver special. But it did. Because what Gulliver did best was finding runaways.

The younger they were, the better at it he was. He understood them, and they understood him. Explaining it to Mia, he'd said, I look on the outside the way they feel on the inside.

Bella Vespucci was older than many of the kids he'd been hired to find over the years. That didn't make things harder. Eighteen-year-old girls had a network of friends. They had credit cards and bank accounts. They bought things. They had cell phones, and they used them. All of that made them easier to trace than younger kids. But one thing was true for all kids, whatever their age. When you are on the street, money runs out fast. Faster than you think possible. And it's when the money runs out that most kids have a choice to make. They can either go back home or find a way to make their way on the street. It was when they chose to stay on the street that things could get ugly—and they often did.

But Gulliver knew better than to make leaps without evidence. He had to start at the beginning and go from there. Tony had left him as much information as he could. Gulliver had all sorts of photos of Bella. He had a list of names of girlfriends and boyfriends. He had a list of addresses and phone numbers. He had bank-account numbers. Credit-card numbers. He had the reports the other private investigators had written up for Joey Vespucci. Gulliver shook his head in sadness. If only the other parents who had hired him to find their kids had cared this much, their kids probably wouldn't have run away to begin with. And they would have been much easier to find.

After reading through the other private eyes' reports, Gulliver called Bella's phone number. It was always the first thing he did if the missing person had a cell phone. Most of the time it didn't work, but every once in a while the missing kid would answer.

Sometimes that was all it took. Sometimes all the kid needed was to hear a kind voice and have a shoulder to cry on. Gulliver's shoulders weren't very big, but they had stood up to many tears. Teenagers were like human lie detectors. They could tell when adults were being real with them or putting them on. And they never doubted Gulliver's honesty. They seemed to sense in his voice that he understood their pain. But this time, Gulliver didn't even get to hear Bella's voice-mail message. Her voice-mail box was full. Of course it was. That wasn't a good sign.

According to Tony, it had been over a month since Joey and Maria had heard from Bella. Bella had been painting since she was a child and was a freshman at the Fashion Institute of Technology on 7th Avenue and West 27th Street in Manhattan.

Joey offered to send her to any art school she wanted to go to, Tony had said.

Here or anywhere. She could have gone to any school—in New York or Paris or Boston or London, if that's what she wanted—but she picked FIT. Can you figure that? A kid of mine as a painter?

A house painter maybe, Gulliver had joked.

Tony had laughed and actually patted Gulliver on the back.

Gulliver didn't say anything at the time, but where Bella had chosen to go to school might prove helpful. Though FIT was a good school, it was part of the State University of New York. Why would a kid with a rich, powerful dad choose to go to a State University school when she could choose any school she wanted?

New York was full of world-famous art schools. Pratt Institute. Columbia University School of the Arts. Parsons School of Design. School of Visual Arts. Cooper Union. Tisch School of the Arts at NYU. Bella had chosen FIT of all those schools. Why? Gulliver thought he might know the answer, but before he went looking for her, there was someone he had to see. He dialed Ahmed Foster's number.

FIVE

Ahmed Foster pulled his Escalade right up to the front gate of Joey Vespucci's mansion on Staten Island. Gulliver had explained the situation to him on the way over. Ahmed was an ex–Navy Seal and Gulliver's unofficial partner in the PI business. Although Gulliver could handle himself, he didn't look like he could. That was never a problem for Ahmed. He was a hard man and built like a linebacker. Agile as a cat, Ahmed had the skills and intimidation factor Gulliver lacked.

"You want me to pull on in or wait out here, little man?" Ahmed asked.

That was another thing about Ahmed. He was one of a very few people who could call Gulliver "little man" and get away with it.

"No, you better wait out here."

Joey "Dollar Menu" Vespucci was two very different men in one body. The face he showed the public and the media was like his nickname and the outside of his house. He meant for people to see him as loud and tough but a bit of a clown. A man with no real style or brains. But the man Gulliver had come to know was not that. The Joey Gulliver knew was both street-smart and just plain smart. He was a man of fine tastes. And he was more than tough. He was deadly, as dangerous as a downed power line in a rain puddle. It was because of this that Gulliver came to him before going out on the street to search for Bella.

Gulliver was smart too. Smart like Joey. Just not as powerful or dangerous. Gulliver understood that once he began looking for Bella, word would leak back to Joey. And that would raise all sorts of questions. Questions like, How did Gulliver find out about Bella? Who asked him to look for her? Questions neither Tony nor Gulliver could risk Joey asking. So Gulliver knew he would have to get Joey's blessing before beginning the search. He had to give Tony, Maria and himself cover while he did his job. The fact was, if he looked for Bella without Joey's blessing, there would be trouble. Gulliver also had his own private reasons for being here. He wanted to show Joey that he was the better man. He wanted to make Joey feel small. Smaller even than himself.

At first sight of Gulliver's small figure hobbling up the long driveway, Tony looked as if he might pass out. But Gulliver knew Tony would catch on. Tony would realize the same things Gulliver had. That they needed Joey to approve of Gulliver's looking for Bella. Gulliver gave a wink to Tony as he came up the stairs onto the big stone porch. Tony gave him a slight nod back. They were on the same page.

"What the hell you doing here, Bug?" Tony said, extra loud in case the boss was nearby or someone else was watching.

"Not to see you, you big moron."

"Watch out, Bug, or I might step on you and squish your little freak guts out all over the porch."

"Don't make me have to make a fool out of you again in front of your boss."

"Screw you," Tony said. "I'll go in and see if the boss feels like dealing with insects today."

A few minutes later, Gulliver Dowd was seated across the big desk from Joey Vespucci. The don smiled at Gulliver.

Before the incident with the envelope, before the choice Joey had forced Gulliver to make between Keisha and Mia, these two men had been friendly. Not friends exactly— even prior to learning of Vespucci's indirect connection to Keisha's murder, Gulliver couldn't be friends with a man of violence. Behind all of Joey's charm and fine tastes was a man who rose to power by killing his rivals. But Joey and Gulliver respected one another, and Gulliver couldn't deny that Joey had been helpful to him in the past.

"After what happened between us on the boardwalk, I didn't think I would ever see you again, little man," Vespucci said, still smiling at the sight of Gulliver across from him. Vespucci was another of the few people who could get away with calling him "little man."

"I didn't think so either, Joey."

"You still drinking vodka?" Vespucci asked.

"The cheaper the better."

Vespucci stood. Went over to the bar. Poured Gulliver a few fingers of vodka. He poured himself a hefty glass of single-malt scotch. Gulliver gave Joey the once-over. The don was still a handsome man in his late fifties or early sixties. But he looked worse for wear. The lines on his face were etched more deeply, and there were more of them. There was a faraway look in his eyes. His hand shook slightly as he poured the drinks.

"To what do I owe the pleasure of seeing you again?" Vespucci asked, handing Gulliver his drink.

"I hear things on the street."

Vespucci made a weak try at laughter. "Things. What kind of things?"

"Things like you've hired some of my business rivals to do what I do better than they do."

"That so? And why would I do that?"

"Because your daughter Bella has been missing for a month," Gulliver said. "And no one can find her."

Vespucci's face conveyed many different emotions at once. The same ones Gulliver had seen on Tony's face earlier that day. The same except for one. Anger. Joey Vespucci was a man who liked being in control. A man who knew things other people didn't know. He liked knowing things before other people knew them. He didn't like it when people knew things they weren't supposed to know. Vespucci really didn't like that Gulliver knew about Bella. That much was clear.

"Who told you that?" he almost growled. "I want a name."

Gulliver shook his head. "No names. Like I said, Joey, I hear things. You forget—this is what I do for a living. I'm the best there is at it. Word gets around. Word gets back. That's all. It's how the street works.

You know that. I have a lot of sources out there. When your guys asked around, people got curious. When I heard, I decided to come to you."

Vespucci guzzled his drink. "Why come to me?"

"Because I'm going to find your daughter."

"Says who?"

Gulliver thumped his own chest. "Says me."

"I don't need you, little man."

"Oh yes you do. More than you know. You need me bad. A month on the streets is a very long time, Joey. It can be a whole lifetime. A man with all your power and contacts hasn't been able to find her."

Vespucci got a sick look on his face, but he was a stubborn man. He hadn't got all this power and kept it by giving in or giving up easily.

"Exactly, Dowd. Even with all the juice and reach I got, I can't find her. What makes you think you can do it?"

"Because I'm the best. And having all the power and contacts in the world won't help you unless you know how to use them. I know how to do that. I have a track record."

Vespucci laughed a mean laugh. "You don't fool me, Dowd. I know your game. You think if you find Bella, I'll spill. That I'll be so grateful, I'll tell you about your sister's murder."

Gulliver shook his head and smiled. "No, Joey. I know you won't tell me, and this isn't a game. I got nothing against your girl. I got nothing against your wife. My problem is with you. But if you want to know why I'm here, I'll tell you."

"Okay, I'll bite. Why are you here?"

"Two reasons. One, I want your blessing. It'll be easier for me to find Bella if I'm not working against other people or looking over my shoulder. If you let me go out there and keep your people out of the way, it will work better, and I'll get to her sooner."

"The other reason?"

"To prove to you that I'm a bigger man than you will ever be. That in spite of what you did to me, I can rise above it. Your girl is who is important here. Not me. Not you. And when you have her back, I'll have the satisfaction of knowing that deep down I'm a good person. That even though I have every reason on earth to hate you, I still did this thing."

"You want money?"

"Keep your money, Joey. I don't want it, and I wouldn't take it if you gave it to me. All I want is the info you got so far. I want you to fire the two yo-yos you hired instead of me. And I want access to all of your contacts and a promise from you to keep your people out of my way. You want to loan me some manpower, then give me Tony."

Vespucci's eyes got big. "You hate each other's guts."

"Right. That way you can keep tabs on me, and I can have a little extra help."

"All right, Dowd. You got a week and you got Tony. Find her."

"I will."

Vespucci put his right hand out for Gulliver to shake, but the little man got off his chair and walked out of the room.

SIX

Ahmed, Tony and Gulliver headed into Brooklyn. Bella's apartment was in Greenpoint. Greenpoint had once been a largely Polish neighborhood, but it had been overrun by hipsters. Williamsburg had gotten too crowded, so the hipsters had moved to the next neighborhood over. Kids no longer wanted to live in Greenwich Village or SoHo. They wanted to live in Brooklyn. Gulliver still couldn't get used to it. When he was growing up on Long Island, no one wanted to live in Brooklyn. Not even the people who lived there.

Now it was the hippest, hottest place in all of New York City. So it was no surprise that the daughter of a rich and powerful man would choose to live there.

"I thought freshmen at state schools had to live in campus dorms," Gulliver said to Tony as Ahmed pulled off the Brooklyn-Queens Expressway.

"They do, but it's Joey Vespucci's daughter we're talking about here," Tony answered.

Gulliver shook his head. "But even Joey can't make all the rules go away. He's a Mafia don, not the governor of the state."

"It was easy." Tony grunted. "When Joey can't break the rules or change them, he goes around them. Just because he's paying the rent on Bella's dorm room don't mean she got to live there, right? So to make sure Bella don't get in no trouble, Joey also pays her roommate's dorm rent too, and everybody's happy. Bella lives where she wants, and the roommate's got her own private dorm room."

Most of the runaways Gulliver had dealt with were from poor families, but not all of them. A fair number had been from well-to-do families. Money didn't make families immune to abuse or violence or bad parenting. Gulliver didn't doubt for a second that Joey and Maria loved Bella. Plus, she had the extra love of her real father, Tony. But love wasn't always enough to protect kids from the demons. Their own and the ones in the world. Sometimes love wasn't nearly enough.

"So what is Bella like, Tony?"

"Why?"

Tony seemed antsy at talking about her in front of Ahmed.

"Don't worry about Ahmed," Gulliver said. "He'll keep your secret. Not because I tell him to. Not because it's his job. Not because he was a Navy Seal."

"Then why?" Tony wanted to know.

Gulliver said, "Because it's his nature. Right, Ahmed?"

Ahmed gave a slight nod of his head and guided the SUV into Greenpoint.

"So tell me what she's like."

But Tony needed another push. "Why? Why does it matter what she's like?"

"It will help us find her, Tony. It could tell us who she might turn to or run from when things go bad. If I know how someone reacts to things, it helps me think like they might think. So please, help me out here."

Tony sighed. "She's real serious about stuff, Dowd. She thinks a lot of deep thoughts. You know what I mean? She don't look at the world like her sisters or her parents. And she liked being with herself while she painted. She has always been her own person. I mean, she's loving and everything. She's even been nice and sweet to me. But she never needed a lot of girlfriends or nothing. She's not sad or a loner. Not like that."

"She's self-contained," Gulliver said. "I know some people like that. Any boyfriends?"

"Not now," Tony said. "There used to be a guy. An artsy-fartsy type she knew from high school."

"Mike Goodwin? I saw his name on the other PI reports."

"That's right, Dowd."

"So what happened with them?"

"They dated for a while and then he went off to school somewheres in Ohio or Michigan or someplace like that."

"Okay," Gulliver said. "When we get to her building, you and Ahmed go have some lunch. I'll talk to the super and the neighbors. You two would scare the piss out of them. I bet that's what happened when Joey's people talked to them."

Neither Ahmed nor Tony objected. They knew Gulliver was right.

"Okay, little man, this is it," Ahmed said as he slowed the Escalade to a stop in front of Bella's building.

"I'll text you when I'm ready."

Gulliver hopped out of the Caddy and waited for them to drive away before he walked to the building entrance. So, he thought, it begins.

SEVEN

Although many of the store signs were still written in Polish, Greenpoint had changed. It was once an area of narrow streets full of row houses crammed tightly together. And down by the East River there were factory buildings and warehouses. A lot of the neighborhood still looked that way. Bella's building fit in like a black puppy in a litter of white kittens. It was a tall, modern high-rise of concrete, steel and glass. Lots and lots of glass. There was so much glass because the building had great views of the Manhattan skyline. Maybe kids liked living here more than across the river, but they liked looking at Manhattan.

Gulliver didn't even need to get buzzed into the building. A couple of hipsters on their way out of the building held the door open for him. They gave him that look as they passed. The look of shock and shame and pity. But Gulliver was immune to it. The important thing was that he had gotten into Bella's building without having to waste time. He went straight to the super's apartment. Knocked on the door. Stood back. If he didn't stand back, the person looking through the peephole wouldn't be able to see him.

The man standing before Gulliver was a heavyset man with an unfriendly, unshaven face. He wore blue coveralls and work boots. He tilted his head at Gulliver. He looked confused and amused at the sight of the little man in the nice clothes.

"What can I do for you?" he asked.

"You can show me apartment 15D." And before the super could protest, Gulliver handed him three twenty-dollar bills.

Five minutes later, the two men were standing at the door of 15D. The super fished through his big key ring and smiled when he found the right one. But when he grabbed the doorknob, it turned and the door opened without need of the key. The super acted surprised. Too surprised to suit Gulliver.

The apartment was a wreck. You could see that from the doorway. Gulliver told the super to stay in the hall. He unholstered his SIG and used his elbow to push the door back. Stepping inside, Gulliver knew things had been stolen. He didn't need to have seen the apartment before. There was a large TV table with no TV on it. A computer desk with no computer on it. A wall unit with empty spaces where a stereo or surround-sound system might have been. When he looked closely at these three places, Gulliver saw outlines in the dust that told him he was right. There had been a TV. A computer. A sound system. Closets were open. Clothes were thrown everywhere. Drawers had been emptied and turned upside down. If there had been jewelry or cash in the apartment when Bella went missing, it was gone now. There was something else. The walls were empty. There were nails and hangers where pictures or photos had been hung, but no pictures or photos.

"You want I should call the cops?" the super asked.

Gulliver shook his head. "No."

The super looked surprised and relieved. It didn't take a genius to figure out what had happened here, but Gulliver kept it to himself for the moment.

"No?" the super repeated. "Are you sure?"

"Very." Then Gulliver said, "You know who rents this apartment?"

"Sure. Pretty girl. An artist, right?"

Gulliver nodded. "You know her name?"

"Vespucci."

"That's right. That name sound familiar to you?" Gulliver asked. He didn't wait for the super to answer. "You know, Vespucci, as in Joey 'Dollar Menu' Vespucci. Like that."

The super got a look on his face like he'd been hit with a pipe across the kidneys.

"Yeah, I don't think Joey would want the cops involved with his youngest daughter's apartment getting robbed," Gulliver said. "He's a man who likes to handle these things on his own."

The super looked about ready to faint.

Then Gulliver delivered the last part of his message. "My guess is that things would go easier on the thief if the stolen stuff got returned. The faster the better. The more that gets returned, the fewer the limbs that will get removed from the thief's body."

The super turned to go, but Gulliver told him to wait.

"In a few minutes two men will buzz you to get let into the building. Let them in and show them up here."

"Yes, sir," said the super. Then he ran toward the elevator.

EIGHT

Ahmed's expression remained the same. Tony's did not. He looked torn between losing his mind or flying off in a rage. Gulliver understood why seeing the state of Bella's apartment would do that to him. But Gulliver couldn't afford to have Tony losing it.

"This isn't what it looks like." Gulliver spoke directly to Tony.

"What are you talking about? The place looks like it was hit by a freakin' twister."

"Trust me, Tony. At least two different events happened here. Maybe three."

"You're nuts, Dowd."

"Nah, Tony," Ahmed said, "the little man is right. He knows his stuff."

Gulliver explained. "Look, I read the reports. When the PIs Joey hired first checked out the apartment, it was fine. It was fine the second time too. In fact, they staked out the building for two weeks straight. Then they took their man off the building, figuring it was a waste of time and manpower. Somebody figured out that Bella was missing and knew this was an easy score. Ten to one it was the super. I'm sure it was him who came in and took the electronics. He also took the jewelry and whatever cash Bella had around."

Tony's face had twisted so that he barely looked human. "I'll kill that mother—"

Gulliver held up his palms. "Relax. I already threw a scare into the super. I guarantee you, whatever he didn't sell off or fence will be returned. And he will replace everything else with newer and bigger models. Besides, he didn't have anything to do with Bella's disappearing. He's not who or what worries me."

"What are you talking about?" Ahmed asked.

"Look at the walls," Gulliver said.

Tony didn't understand. "What about them?"

Ahmed got it. "They're empty. Nothing's on them."

"Give the man a cigar," Gulliver said. "There had to be pictures and photos on the walls. Maybe even some of Bella's own art."

"Jeez! You're right," Tony said. "The walls used to be full of photos Bella took and things she'd painted. There were family photos and framed museum posters too."

"The super didn't steal those," Gulliver said. "They wouldn't have any value to him."

"So who you think took the stuff off the walls, little man?"

"Good question, Ahmed. Maybe Bella. Maybe she ran away but couldn't stand to be without her work or photos of her family. Some people get attached to objects. I've tracked down grown women who'd been missing since they were young teenagers. Some were living rough. Some were turning tricks. But still I'd find them with little things they'd taken with them—a stuffed penguin or a favorite doll or blanket. Maybe Bella had a friend come in and grab the stuff."

"That's two events, Dowd," Tony said. "You mentioned there might be three."

Gulliver nodded. "I did. Something else is missing too. All of Bella's painting equipment. You can see paint spatter where she used to work in the spare bedroom. But there's no easel. No brushes. No paint. Nothing."

Ahmed smiled. Tony noticed.

"What's your pal smiling at, Dowd?"

"You tell him, Ahmed."

"Like the little man says, the electronics and cash were lifted by the super or whoever. Everything else looks like your girl ran away. Who's going to steal photos and art equipment? At least, that's what it's meant to look like."

"You understand what he means, Tony?" Gulliver asked.

"That if someone wanted us to think Bella left of her own free will, they would take the stuff on the walls and her painting stuff."

Gulliver nodded.

"Now what?" Tony wanted to know.

"Now we've got to find a way to hack Bella's texts, phone messages and computer."

Tony laughed. "Is that all?"

Gulliver said, "Don't worry about it. I've got her phone number and carrier.

You find out who her Internet service was through. Then I'll take care of it."

"She had a Gmail account and one from the local cable company. I seen some of her emails to Maria," Tony said. Then he laughed again. "What are you, Superman in a little package? You're a black belt. You shoot. You handle a knife like you was born with one in your hand. You track down missing people like a bloodhound. You're a genius hacker too?"

"No, but I know one. It'll cost you and Joey big bucks. But unless you want to go to the police, it's your only choice."

"No cops," Tony said. "Joey will never go to the cops. Never!"

"Okay then. Ahmed, you and Tony go have a talk with the super about the security cameras at the building's entrance and exit doors. Make sure he knows that no is not an answer we want to hear. Have all the video for the last two weeks sent to my email address. I'll look around here a little more. Then drop me back at the office. After that, take Tony back to Staten Island. We've got a big day ahead of us tomorrow."

"Come on, Dowd," Tony protested. "It's not that late. Every day that passes—"

"Believe me, Tony, I get it," Gulliver said. "I know you're scared, and you're not used to being scared. But we have to be smart about this. If Bella didn't run, then someone might have her. And if someone has her, we have to assume that person is pretty smart."

"Why?"

"Because he made it look like she came back for her things," Ahmed answered. "Look at the door. It ain't been busted in. Whoever came in here had a key. We figure the super had a key to steal the goods. But whoever came back for the photos and the art stuff had a key too. Most likely Bella's key.

And if Bella didn't run herself, that means whoever has her knows we may be watching for him. He may be watching us. So if anything, we have to look like we think she ran away. We can't be looking desperate or panicked or nothing."

"But if somebody's got her, why ain't Joey got a note asking for money?" Tony asked.

It was a logical question. A question Gulliver didn't want to answer but had to.

"Because sometimes it's not about the money, Tony. It's about the girl." Gulliver patted him on the forearm. "But let's not jump to the wrong ideas here. Let's see what we can find. Just remember that we can't let anyone watching us think we've caught on. Now, go speak to the super. He's already pretty scared. One look at you two, and he'll give you anything you ask for."

When Ahmed and Tony had left, Gulliver took another look around the apartment. He stared out at the Manhattan skyline as night began to fall. It was always an amazing sight, but Gulliver took no comfort in it. He had a bad feeling about this case. A very bad feeling.

NINE

Only two people on earth knew the real identity of the hacker known as Happy Meal. One was Gulliver Dowd. The other was Happy Meal himself. Happy Meal's real name was Sha'wan Jones. Most folks just called him Shea, like the old stadium the Mets used to play in. And to most folks, Shea was a twentysomething slacker living in the basement of his mom's house in Bed-Stuy. But Gulliver Dowd wasn't most folks. Not only did Gulliver know Happy Meal's identity. He also knew that the house belonged to Happy Meal, not to his mom.

It was Gulliver who had found Shea out on the street almost eight years earlier. Shea was one of Gulliver's first runaway cases. His mother couldn't pay much, but Gulliver was trying to get a rep back then. A good rep was more important than money when you were starting out. As a chubby black fourteen-year-old kid with Asperger's who didn't play ball, Shea was bullied, beaten and robbed at school. Gulliver Dowd knew something about that. Yes, he did. With no dad at home and a mom who loved him but worked two jobs, Shea was left to deal with his problems by himself. One day he just ran.

Gulliver had located him in a few days. Shea was already in bad shape. He was eating out of garbage cans on the streets of the Bronx. When Gulliver found him, the first thing Shea asked for was a Happy Meal. Gulliver drove him to a McDonald's and bought him two. The nickname had stuck.

Everything else had changed. Sha'wan Jones had grown into a lanky young man. Handsome too. He hadn't outgrown the Asperger's, but he had learned to deal with it and use it. These days Happy Meal's services were in big demand, and he made a boatload of money. Most of what he did wasn't exactly legal. He didn't steal money or plant viruses or malware. He didn't destroy systems. He was good at peeking in places he wasn't allowed and figuring things out. He could see things everyone else missed.

When Gulliver went down into the basement, Shea didn't stand to greet him. He just sort of half smiled at Gulliver and kept pecking at his keyboard. He never took his eyes off the screen.

He did say, "Did you bring it?"

Gulliver laughed. He raised up his right hand to show Shea the bag with the Happy Meal in it.

Shea nodded. He didn't eat burgers or fries anymore. But this was their ritual. Rituals were important to Shea. And this was the way Gulliver and Shea hugged hello.

"I've got a program working on the video you sent me from the building. I'm working on the phone and the computer stuff now. I should have the phone stuff first. Maybe by tomorrow. The computer stuff is more iffy. Depends how much was stored in the cloud."

"Do the best you can."

"I always do, Mr. Dowd." He had never gotten out of the habit of calling Gulliver that.

"I know you do. Any luck locating the phone?"

Shea shook his head. "My guess is that it's been destroyed. Probably in pieces in the river."

Gulliver agreed.

"You think someone's taken her?" Shea asked.

"My gut tells me yes."

"That's good enough for me. Have you told the family yet?"

"Not yet," Gulliver said. "I need something more than my gut for that. These are serious people."

Shea understood without having to ask.

"How much for the work?" Gulliver asked. "My client can afford it, so don't hold back."

Shea shook his head violently. Most of the time he didn't charge Gulliver.

Gulliver knew better than to argue. "When you have something, anything, let me know."

"Will do, Mr. Dowd."

"Anything else, Shea?"

"Did you bring apple juice or milk with my meal?"

"Milk, of course," Gulliver said.

Shea stopped typing and got a weird look on his face.

Gulliver laughed. "Got ya! I brought you apple juice, like always."

That was the one thing Shea still enjoyed from the Happy Meal. As soon as he knew it was apple juice, Shea went back to work.

TEN

The girl sitting across from Gulliver was striking. Thin but curvy, she had light-brown hair cut short in a kind of one-sided bob. She had a triangular face with a well-defined chin. Depending on the light or the angle at which she held her head, the color of her eyes seemed to shift from light blue to green. Her skin was pale and lightly freckled, and her nose was small and angular. She was dressed with great style.

Walking the block-long campus of the Fashion Institute of Technology, Gulliver had noticed it wasn't like most college campuses.

He had also noticed that the students didn't look like most college students. None of them looked as if they had just rolled out of bed. When Gulliver was in college, everyone looked like an unmade bed. Then again, FIT did have the word *fashion* in its name. Its students seemed to take that to heart.

Niki Philipps brushed her hair back and gave Gulliver a cute smile. She hadn't reacted at all when she saw him. That was unusual. Almost everybody but the blind reacted in some way to their first sight of Gulliver Dowd. Niki was Bella's roommate, and she had been happy to accept Joey Vespucci's offer to pay her rent. She said she hadn't thought twice about the offer and didn't see anything wrong with it.

She shrugged her square shoulders. "My folks don't have a lot of money, and this makes it much easier for them. It also means I didn't have to take out a loan this year.

Even though I live on campus and have the food plan, it costs a lot to live in this city."

Gulliver couldn't argue with that. He asked her what she thought of Bella.

"I liked Bella when I met her, and I would have been happy to have her around all the time. She has a real sense of style that has nothing to do with fashion."

"I don't understand," said Gulliver.

"A lot of the kids here are fashion kids. But Bella's style seems to come from inside her. She's serious and deep. When she looks at things, you can just tell she sees them differently than other people do. Like she can see inside them."

Gulliver nodded. He got it. He had that knack too.

"I think we would have been friends if we had the chance. I would have learned a lot from her."

"Maybe you'll still have that chance, Niki."

"I hope so. Are you going to find her, Mr. Dowd?"

"I usually do find who I'm looking for."

She got a worried look on her face. "But not always?"

"No, Niki. Not always."

She thought about that for a second. "How can I help?"

"How long did Bella live here before she stopped pretending?"

"About a week. Just long enough so that if anyone checked, she was cool. But even after she moved out, she would still hang out here sometimes between classes and stuff. We didn't have the same schedule because we aren't in the same major, but we would run into each other now and then. Why?"

"If someone was stalking her, it might have taken that person a while to figure out she wasn't living here."

Niki shuddered as if she had the chills. "Stalking her! That freaks me out."

"Did she ever mention that to you? That there was someone hanging around her? Did you ever see anyone in the lobby or in the halls who didn't belong or made you feel strange?"

Niki's face changed almost at once, but she didn't speak right away. It was as if she wasn't sure if what she had thought of meant anything.

"Don't edit yourself, Niki. Tell me anything, even if it seems foolish or unimportant. Let me judge it. Okay?"

"Well, there was this one time…" Her voice trailed off. She shook her head. "No, it's silly."

"You're right, it's probably nothing. Tell me anyway."

"One day last term. In October, I think. There was a man just outside the entrance to the dorm. And when I was coming into the building, he walked up to me. He said he knew I was Bella's roommate and that he had something for her."

"Something?"

"A note for her," Niki said. "He asked if I could please give it to her. He said it was important and that he would really appreciate it."

"What happened?"

She made a face. Shrugged. "It was just a note in an envelope. I told him I would give it to her when I saw her. He thanked me and left. But she had already moved into her own place by then, so it sat on her bed for about a week. I wasn't in the room when she picked it up. I don't even know when she got it or if she read it. I just looked over at the bed one day, and the envelope was gone."

"And she never mentioned it to you?" Gulliver asked.

"No. Never. But like I said, we only ran into each other now and then. She never asked me where it came from. She just never said anything."

"Is it okay if I ask about the man who gave the envelope to you?"

Niki said, "Sure. Why not?"

"Old or young?"

"Older. Maybe sixty or a little older, I guess."

"Hair?"

"Long and gray. Kind of straggly."

"Eye color?"

Niki thought about that. "Blue. Dark blue. And his skin had lines in it. His cheeks were very thin. He was nice, though, Mr. Dowd. He wasn't, like, crazy or anything. He was kind of like a nice grandfather."

"Anything else?" Gulliver asked.

"He had stained teeth, like he smoked."

"How did he—"

"Wait. His hands were stained too, but not yellow. They were speckled with paint maybe."

"That's great, Niki. You're doing great. How did he speak? Did he have a foreign accent or a strange voice or anything like that?"

"No. At least, not that I can remember," she said, almost disappointed.

Gulliver thanked Niki and got ready to leave, but he had one more thing he was dying to ask her. "Niki, can I ask you a question that's not about Bella?"

"Sure, Mr. Dowd."

"When you saw me for the first time, you didn't react at all. Most people do, you know. When they see how small I am. When they see my body's kind of strange. Most people's eyes get big. Their faces change, or they force themselves to look blank. But not you. Why?"

She looked like she wanted to say something but was holding back.

"You can say anything to me, Niki. You won't hurt my feelings, no matter what it is. I promise."

"We're all kind of freaks here, Mr. Dowd. We're the fashion kids or the art kids. We all feel different here. To me you don't seem so different."

"Thanks for telling me that," he said and turned to go.

"Mr. Dowd. There's something else."

"Something else?"

"About the man who gave me the note."

"What about him?"

"He had style. Flair. He had a brown fedora on, with the front brim turned down, and a camel-hair coat, single-breasted. And he had a nice silk scarf. But none of the clothes were new. They looked…I don't know. Lived in."

"If I could show you a photo of him, would you remember him?"

"I would."

"Thanks again, Niki."

"I hope you find her. Will you tell me what happens, Mr. Dowd? No matter what?"

"I will. I promise."

Gulliver left the dorm and headed back into Brooklyn. On the subway, he thought about the man and the note. He wondered if they had anything to do with Bella's vanishing. He thought about how none of the people Joey Vespucci had hired had bothered talking to Niki. They'd just assumed since Bella had her own place that her "roommate" didn't matter. It wasn't always the little things that mattered. But it often was. You had to look at even the stuff that didn't make sense.

ELEVEN

Ahmed and Tony were waiting for Gulliver at his office when he got back to Red Hook. Both looked antsy. Like they had been pacing as they waited. Like they had something to tell Gulliver. He was right. They both started talking before he was two feet inside the office.

"Ahmed first," Gulliver said.

"Heard some stuff about the boyfriend," he said.

"Good. How about you, Tony?"

"There was some guy who used to hang out around her building in Greenpoint.

I spoke to almost everybody in the building. Took me all freakin' day."

"Let me guess," Gulliver said. "Older man with gray hair and a brown hat. Thin but nice. Polite."

The shock on Tony's face was answer enough. Gulliver was right.

"First let's hear what Ahmed has to say about the boyfriend. Mike Goodwin is his name, right?"

"That's right, little man. Friends say the breakup got kind of ugly. He wanted them to still see only each other even though they'd both be away at different schools."

"But Bella wasn't having any of that. Was she?"

Ahmed shook his head. "No way. Let's just say the boyfriend didn't like Bella saying no to him. I mean, the boy ain't stupid enough to get physical with Joey Vespucci's little girl. But he said some things in front of people. You know what I'm saying?"

Tony asked, "What kind of things?"

"Like, how if he couldn't have her nobody should have her. You know, things along that line."

Tony's face turned a bright red. The veins popped out of his neck. He clenched and unclenched his fists.

Gulliver said, "Tony, relax. Be cool. I know what you're thinking. But he's a kid, and kids say all sorts of stupid stuff they don't mean. A lot of the time they blurt stuff out because they're angry or hurt. Come on. You were a kid once. When Nina broke up with me in high school, I wanted to strike out at her. Mostly, though, I wanted to strike out at myself."

"So you're saying it's not the boyfriend?" Tony was confused.

"No, what I'm saying is don't jump to conclusions without proof. Why don't you and Ahmed go have a talk with the family about their boy. Tony, you've met the kid, right? Be nice. Be respectful. Explain things. Find out as much as you can about him. I'll have someone do some online work about him. We don't want to waste time looking at the kid if he hasn't even been back in New York to do anything. If need be, one of us will go out to his school and have a talk with him. But first things first."

"What about the older guy?" Ahmed asked.

Gulliver detailed his conversation with Niki Philipps.

"Seems pretty harmless," Gulliver said, "but you never know. When I get the breakdown of the video from Bella's building, we'll see." He paused.

"Tony," he said, his voice grave.

"Yeah, what?"

"Are any of Joey's rivals so pissed at him or crazy enough that they would snatch his girl?"

When Tony didn't answer right away, Gulliver got a sick feeling in his belly.

Tony bowed his head. "I guess. A few of the young guys, they watch *The Godfather* and *Goodfellas* and think that's how it should be now. They think Joey's an old man who's gone soft and don't let them earn. But I don't think any of them is stupid enough to try something with… Joey's kids." The phrase stuck in Tony's throat. "But the foreign gangs, they're something else. Of course, you got the Colombians, the Russians and the Chinese gangs, but we have peace with them most of the time. There are other gangs now. New gangs from new countries. We got the Bulgarians, the Chechens, even some Arab gangs. Could be one of them maybe."

"Get me some names and addresses by tomorrow," Gulliver said.

Tony nodded. "Then you and me will go see them?"

"Just me, Tony. You there would be like a red cape in front of a bull. I don't want to start trouble. If there is trouble, I want to end it."

Gulliver knew Tony didn't like that. But he knew, too, that over the years Tony had learned how to deal with things he didn't like.

"Okay, Dowd," was all Tony said.

TWELVE

He sensed the trouble coming out of the darkness before he was even aware of it. He ducked. Swoosh! Crack! Gulliver had had a baseball bat swung at his head before, so he knew the feeling. He felt the rush of air over his head and heard the aluminum smack against the brick of his building. Without thinking, he placed his right palm flat on the pavement. Anchored, he thrust out his left leg and connected. The kick didn't hit his attacker's knee flush, but it was enough to throw off his second swing of the bat.

Gulliver heard the man stumble backward and moan in pain.

Sometimes that was all it took. You got your opponent off-balance. You made him miss a few times, and he retreated. Not this time. Before Gulliver could right himself, his attacker was coming back at him for a third swing. He saw the metal flash. Instead of ducking, he sidestepped it. Strike three! As he sidestepped, he reached under his jacket and unholstered his SIG. Though Gulliver already had a bullet in the chamber, he racked the slide of his semiautomatic. While the racking of the slide wasn't as effective as the cha-ching of a pump-action shotgun, it did tend to get people's attention.

"Holy crap!" the attacker screamed. "Screw this!"

The next thing Gulliver heard was the clink of the aluminum bat falling to the sidewalk. That was followed in short order by the sound of feet running in the other direction. Gulliver supposed he could have shot in the direction of the footfalls and hit the man who had attacked him. But you didn't shoot a gun in the city unless you had no other choice. Only gangsters or fools took that risk. It was too dangerous. There were people and hard surfaces everywhere. Bullets could ricochet. The chances of hitting an innocent person were too great.

When the fight-or-flight tension had left his body, Gulliver tried to piece together the details of the attack. He closed his eyes and controlled his breathing as his sensei had taught him. As he relaxed, he asked himself questions. What did he remember about his attacker? Not about the weapon, but the man who had swung it. Not much. Could he remember what the man was wearing? Too dark. But he did remember two smells. The stink of old cigarettes and the sickly sweet smell of cheap after-shave. In fact, those odors still hung in the air around him. Gulliver smiled to himself, because he had a good idea who had wielded the bat. And since he had the bat, it might be easy to prove.

He holstered his weapon. He bent down and picked up the bullet that had been ejected from his SIG. But as he picked up the bat by the barrel, Gulliver felt sad. He thought again about the attack. What would have happened if he had been killed and never got a chance to see Mia again? What if he never got a chance to say the things to her he still had to say to her? What if they never got to live the life they were meant to live together?

When he got to his custom-made van, he placed the bat in a plastic garbage bag. He turned the key and was about to give a voice command to call Mia when his phone rang. The name and number that flashed onto the screen in his dashboard made him smile. It was Mia calling him. Sometimes the universe is like that.

"I was just going to call you," he said.

"Really?"

"Really. How are you?"

"Okay, I guess," she said.

As happy as he was to hear from her, Gulliver didn't like the way her voice sounded.

"What's wrong, Mia?"

"I can't do this anymore, Gullie."

"I know. I've been an idiot, and this is all my fault."

"I'm not interested in blame. I'm just lonely. It's not the same living here without you."

"Then I'll come home...tonight. Right now!"

But if Gulliver thought Mia would jump at the idea, he was wrong. There was a long pause before she spoke. And when she did, she said the last words he wanted to hear.

"No, Gullie. I've made a decision."

His heart thumped so hard he swore he could see his jacket moving on his chest. "A decision?"

"I'm moving back to Michigan. It's too painful for me to live here anymore. I just want to go home and have a normal life."

There, she'd said it. She'd said the one word that was like kryptonite to him. Normal. If there was one thing Gulliver Dowd could never be, it was normal. If there was one thing he could never give someone, it was a normal life. He had accepted these things about himself even before he had overcome his bitterness. Even before Keisha had been murdered. Normal wasn't in his deck of playing cards. His deck was fifty-two jokers.

"Please, Mia, don't," he said, fighting back tears.

"I gave my two weeks' notice at the clinic today. It will take some time to get all my other stuff settled, but a month from now I'll be home in Roseville. I didn't want you to hear it from someone else, and I didn't know when I'd see you again."

"But I love you."

"I love you too, Gulliver Dowd. You're the best man I've ever met. I don't think I'll ever meet anyone like you again."

"But if we love each other—"

She cut him off. "Sometimes love's not enough, Gullie. I guess this is one of those times."

Then she was gone.

Gulliver looked at the bat in the plastic bag on his backseat. He half wished he hadn't ducked. More than half.

THIRTEEN

Gulliver had the bat in his hand when he strode into the offices of Kid Finders, Inc. Stevie Flax was sitting behind his desk, smoking a cigarette. He acted as if all was good with the world and he didn't have a care. As if he was happy to see the little man standing in front of him, baseball bat in hand.

"What you got there, Dowd?"

"What's it look like, Stevie?"

"Baseball bat," said Flax. "Want some coffee?"

"Sure."

Flax went over to the coffeepot. Poured a cup for Gulliver. Gave it to him. Pointed to the milk and sugar.

"You thinking of taking up baseball, Dowd? Given that you're such a shrimp, I suppose it's better than basketball or football. You'll sure walk a lot."

"Nah, Stevie, I'm here to give it back to you," Gulliver said. He sipped his coffee. "Jeez, this stuff is terrible." He put the cup down.

"I know. It's from yesterday. I save it for company I don't like or didn't invite over. And what's this about giving the bat back to me? I've never seen it before in my life."

"No, huh? I guess we're going to do this the hard way. You aren't going to like the hard way. Because as big as you are, I'm still going to kick your ass all over this office." Gulliver smiled a cruel smile. "The best part of it is, there won't be a thing you can do about it. And let me tell you something, Stevie.

I came in here hoping you would deny you came after me last night. You know why? I'll tell you why. Because the woman I love told me she's leaving me, and I'm in the mood to take that out on someone. And you just volunteered for the job."

"Wait! Wait!" Flax yelled, putting his palms up. "I swear, I got no idea what you're talking about. On my mother's soul."

"You swear, huh?"

"I swear."

Gulliver said, "Funny, because the guy who swung this bat at me last night wears the same cheap aftershave as you do. He smells of old cigarette smoke the way you do."

"Wasn't me. I swear."

"Yeah, you keep saying that. One quick way to prove it."

"How's that?" Flax asked, then laughed a nervous laugh.

Before Flax could blink, Gulliver had dropped the bat. A knife appeared in his misshapen hand. He was on Flax. There was a ripping sound. The sound of denim shredding. Then it was Gulliver laughing. He was laughing because Flax looked silly with his right pant leg slit open to his thigh.

"Hell of a bruise you got there, Stevie. Odd thing is, I kicked the guy who attacked me last night. Kicked him right there where that bruise of yours is," Gulliver said, pointing at the ugly purple mark. "I bet if I looked close enough, I'd find the imprint of my boot heel in the bruise. Should I look and see?"

Flax shook his head

"I didn't think so. I know Joey Vespucci fired your ass. I told him to. But coming after me was stupid, Stevie. I may just have to tell Joey what you did last night. I hear his guys have a fondness for using baseball bats. You ever see the movie *Casino*? Remember what happened to Joe Pesci and his brother?"

Flax turned white and fell back into the nearest chair. "I needed this job, Dowd. I'm broke."

"Then maybe you should stop playing the ponies and going down to Atlantic City. Very stupid of you to try and soak a guy like Joey Vespucci. When I read your report, I could tell you were jerking him around. He would have caught on sooner or later. Getting you fired probably saved your life. How much are you into the shylocks for?"

"Thirty grand."

"When this is over, I'll see what I can do for you. Then maybe you can come work for me. In the meantime, go get yourself some help."

"Whatever you say, Dowd. Whatever you say."

But as Gulliver left Flax's office, he knew nothing would come of it. Flax would only get deeper in debt. He'd spend the rest of his life trying to pay back the vig without ever cutting into the real debt. Some men were born to lose.

FOURTEEN

Tony met Gulliver at a diner on Coney Island Avenue. Gulliver pushed his eggs around the plate. Tony had no such trouble. He ate with gusto.

"What's with you?" Tony asked.

"Mia's moving back to Michigan."

"Why?"

"Because...forget it. It's a long story, and it involves your boss. It involves the fee you're going to give me when I find Bella."

"You're an idiot. You know that, Dowd?"

Gulliver looked up from his plate. His face was red and twisted. "Am I?"

"Yeah. You are. Love don't come around like the hands on a clock. Sometimes it only comes around once. Sometimes never. Only came once for me. After Maria, that was it. I been with plenty of women since, and I ain't found love again. I almost thought I did, but when me and Maria had that thing all those years ago…it reminded me what love really is. Bella is a reminder of that. Of what love can produce. You had it twice. And let's be real here, Dowd. Handsome as you are, that's pretty lucky. You ain't exactly a prize."

"A booby prize maybe."

They both laughed.

"Do whatever you got to do to keep her, Dowd. Don't let her go home. Without love, nothing else is worth it. Nothing."

Gulliver changed the subject. "You got that list for me?"

"Yeah, I got it." Tony slid a piece of lined paper across the table. "So you and me going to go see these guys?"

Gulliver shook his head. "You're half right. I'm going to see them. Just me. Like how I showed up at Joey's that first time. No one ever sees me as a threat. I get into places you couldn't get into with an Abrams tank."

"Whatever you say, Dowd."

"So did you and Ahmed talk to Mike Goodwin's family?" Gulliver asked.

"Yeah. Dead end."

"You sure?"

"The kid went to school and, like, fell in love with this other girl about a week into their first term. He's only been home twice since he left for Michigan last August. Spends his holidays with the girl and her family in California. Goodwin's folks say the girl's dad is a Hollywood big shot and sends his private jet to bring his girl and the Goodwin kid back to Palm Springs all the time. Ahmed googled the father, and it seems the father checks out. Like I said, I think the boyfriend is a dead end."

"Okay, I think we'll have a better idea of things by tonight," Gulliver said. "You and Ahmed go talk to Bella's professors at FIT. Talk to her classmates. See if that gets you anywhere. If it doesn't, go talk to everyone in her building again."

Tony rolled his eyes. "But we already talked to everyone in her building, and didn't you talk to the professors and staff when you went to talk to that Philipps girl?"

"No one said this was exciting work, but that's how it's done."

"Okay. Whatever."

Gulliver threw a twenty and a ten on the table. But as he hopped down off the booth cushion, Tony grabbed him by his right bicep.

"Don't let her go, Dowd. You let Mia go, she won't come back." Then Tony released his grip.

Gulliver left the diner without saying another word, but he knew Tony was right.

FIFTEEN

Gulliver was exhausted by the time he'd worked his way into Flushing, Queens. Flushing began as a Dutch colony. It was best known to baseball fans as the home of the Mets, but these days its population was largely Asian. It rivaled the Chinatowns in Manhattan and in Sunset Park, Brooklyn, and was also home to a huge Korean population. Without a doubt, it was home too to some of the best Asian food in all of New York City. And that was really saying something. But Gulliver wasn't hungry. He was not here for soup dumplings or kimchi.

He was here to see Gun Park. No joke. No play on words.

According to Tony, Gun Park was the head of Gangpae in New York City. Gangpae was the South Korean Mafia. Of all the newer gangs in New York, Gangpae had the biggest conflict with the old New York mob. The trouble had to do with the transport of electronics and garments from the New Jersey docks, Newark Airport and Kennedy Airport. Along with carting and construction, the trucking of cargo had long been controlled by the Mafia. There was a time when even asking the wrong kind of question about those businesses could get a man's leg broken. Sometimes much worse. But with the RICO Act, the government had badly weakened the old mob. The Mafia's rep no longer scared new players.

If Gulliver had not believed that before, he did now. He had spent most of his day walking into the dens of the most powerful organized-crime bosses in New York City. The storeroom of a Syrian food store on Atlantic Avenue. A Chinese teahouse on Mott Street. A Dominican bar in Washington Heights. A Bulgarian social club on Ditmars Boulevard. The reactions he got were the usual. A mixture of curious stares, annoyance and laughter. The laughter came to an end when Gulliver kicked someone's ass. Or pulled out his SIG. Or his knife. But come to an end it did. After that he was treated with respect for his courage and skill.

All the gangsters he met with agreed that they had issues with the old New York mob. Some of them laughed at it, as if the Mafia were a quaint relic like a rotary phone or a TV set with a picture tube. None of them felt the least bit threatened by the old mob. Gulliver suspected that these guys talked braver than they really were. But he wasn't there to argue with them. Only to find out if they were angry enough with

Joey Vespucci to grab his daughter. Most of them got pretty angry when Gulliver mentioned the possibility.

We don't make war on the children of our enemies, they told him.

Gulliver believed them. They all offered to help in any way they could to find Bella. Gulliver believed that less. But even if he had, he wouldn't have taken them up on the offer. It didn't always help to have more people beating the brush. Sometimes it was better to have fewer people, who knew what they were doing. This was one of those times.

Now here he was in Flushing, but this time there were no fights. No one pulled a weapon. All Gulliver did was ask to see Mr. Park. It seemed as if they were expecting him. They might have been, for all he knew. Word spreads.

After patting Gulliver down and taking his weapons, a man in his thirties showed him into the office at the rear of a Korean grocery store. The man who escorted him was strapped, but Gulliver doubted the man would need to use his weapon in most situations. He had the air of a serious man. A man not to be toyed with.

The rear of the store was full of magical smells. Garlic. Peppers. Vinegar and spices Gulliver did not know. Without being told, he removed his boots and left them on the threshold of the office, next to a pair of fine-quality handmade Italian loafers. The office was larger than he expected. It was beautifully decorated. The deep red carpeting alone must have cost several thousand dollars. There was an ornate wooden desk, and lovely wood paneling on the walls. Inside the office was a man about Joey Vespucci's age. He was dressed in khakis, a beige cashmere sweater and brown socks. He was putting golf balls into a regulation golf hole cut into the carpet. Gulliver waited, not saying anything.

When the ball clanged into the dead center of the cup, Gun Park smiled ever so slightly. He hit the next ball with the same result. Again the same smile that quickly vanished. As he prepared to hit the next ball, he looked at Gulliver's stockinged feet and nodded in approval. There was no smile.

He said, "You have had a busy day, Mr. Dowd. Can I get you something to eat or drink? Tea? A beer?"

Gulliver thought about it. He knew better than to reject an offer of hospitality from a powerful person. In many cultures, it is an insult to do so.

"A cold beer would be great. Thank you."

"Please sit." Park gestured to a pile of colorful silk cushions at a low table toward the rear of the large office.

He called to the man who had showed Gulliver into the room and then came to the table and sat across from Gulliver.

"You are a curious man, Mr. Dowd," Park said. "You are a very hard man but a generous one. Koreans honor these things. Korea is a hard land, but we are a generous, caring people."

At that moment Park's man came in with a bottle of beer—OB Lager—and a glass. He placed them in front of Gulliver. Gulliver thanked him and nodded but didn't touch the bottle or the glass. He knew he was being tested. With men like Park, everything was a test and everything else was about respect.

"You asked for the beer, yet you don't touch it," Park said. "Why so?"

"Because it would be impolite for a guest to pour his own drink."

"I like you more and more, Mr. Dowd." Park poured Gulliver's beer and then gestured for him to have some.

He did, and it went down well. "May I speak frankly, Mr. Park?"

"Please do."

"You know why I am here."

Park nodded. "Of course."

"Then may I ask if you have Mr. Vespucci's daughter?"

Park did not answer directly. "Koreans value their children greatly. But every man you have seen today has said the same thing. Have they not?"

Gulliver nodded.

"They would. We all say things that one part of our hearts believes. But there is another part of our hearts that knows that we in this business value other things more. There are things Mr. Vespucci has done. Things all these other men have done. Things I have done that would put lies to all the lofty things we say we value. But we are men who value more greatly power, fear, respect and wealth. There is no limit on the things we would do in order to attain and keep that which we prize."

Gulliver said, "I know that, sir. That is why I have come to you."

"You do not value these things, Mr. Dowd?"

Gulliver laughed. "I mean no disrespect, Mr. Park. I laugh because the question has no meaning to me. Do you know Shakespeare, *Richard III*?"

"I do. A horse! a horse! my kingdom for a horse!"

"Exactly. All the money and power in the world could not change the man that looks back at me from the mirror each morning. So of what value would they be to me?"

Park thought about that for several seconds. "If I thought we could somehow gain what we wanted from Mr. Vespucci by taking his daughter, we would. But we do not think that." Park did not smile, but there was a sudden warmth in his eyes. "We do not have his daughter. I have only the sincerest hope that you can return her safely to her family. I will not disrespect you by offering unwanted help, Mr. Dowd. Please know that you are always welcome here." The warmth in his eyes vanished. "Now, if you would leave me to my golf."

Night had fallen on New York by the time Gulliver got back to his van. As he was about to get inside, his phone rang. It was Happy Meal.

"Hey, Shea. What's up?"

"Get over here," Shea said in his flat-toned voice. "Get over here right now. And you don't have to stop for a Happy Meal."

SIXTEEN

Gulliver got from Flushing to Bed-Stuy as fast as he could. He skidded to a stop in front of Shea's brownstone and hobbled down to the basement as fast as his uneven little legs would carry him.

"What is it?" Gulliver asked, out of breath.

"That was fast, Mr. Dowd."

"As long as I don't have to run, I can be quick." The joke was lost on Shea. "So, what's so urgent?"

Shea pointed at a big monitor on a desk next to his work station. "Pull up a chair over there and keep your eyes on the monitor."

Gulliver did as the hacker supreme instructed.

"Bella's phone is definitely a dead end. It's probably at the bottom of Sheepshead Bay, and I didn't find much in her texts either," Shea said. "There were some texts from a guy in her art-history class that I think were flirty, but it's hard for me to know. And there were some graphic texts from two girls in her figure-drawing class. They mentioned wanting…wanting to be with her."

"Should we check them out?"

"I don't think so. Unless I'm totally wrong."

"Where are you going with this?" Gulliver pushed.

"I'm not sure yet, so just follow me for a few minutes."

Gulliver knew he had no choice. Shea worked in his own rigid way, and you either went with it or not at all. "Sorry. Go ahead."

"There wasn't much in her email account that on its own would get anyone's attention either," Shea continued. "But when I was digging around, I found this. Look at your screen, Mr. Dowd."

An image flashed onto the monitor. It was the home page for a website called bellartgirl.com. At the top of the page were the headings "Home," "About Bellartgirl," "FAQ," "Gallery" and "Sales." Below the headings and set against a dark-green backdrop was the image of a wildly colorful painting. Red. Orange. Black. Deep blue. Neon green. There were drips and splatters. Droplets and sprays. Thick lines and shadows. Circles and squares. It was very good but looked like a combination of paintings done by famous artists.

"Click on 'Gallery,'" Shea said.

And when Gulliver did, he was amazed to see the wide range of Bella's work. He was impressed. She had done figure drawing. Sculpture. Photography. Mostly she had painted—and in very different styles. Some of her paintings were almost like photos. Others were like the home-page cover image. Daring and splashy. Some were portraits. Some were landscapes. Some were street scenes. Some were still lifes.

Gulliver knew some of the people in the portraits. Maria. Bella's sisters. There was even one of Tony, looking tired and glum. There were none of Joey. There wouldn't be. Not for sale, at least. All were well done, but all had that young-artist feel. The feel of a girl trying to discover her own style and voice by copying others. Gulliver had no artistic talent himself. Yet he understood that you found your own voice and style by first copying others.

"Okay," he said. "So Bella was talented. She wanted to sell her stuff, and she set up a website to do it. There must be thousands of sites like this all over the Internet. Kids who want to sell their art or their T-shirts or whatever. But does it get us anywhere?"

"We're almost there, Mr. Dowd. The domain name is still hers, and the hosting fee has been prepaid for five years. There are still two years left on that. But the site hasn't been active for at least two years. Click on 'About Bellartgirl.' Look at her image. Look at her bio."

Gulliver did so. Bella was a smart girl. She wanted to sell her work and get it out into the world. But she also knew she could not do it as the girl of a Mafia don. So there was no photograph of her. Only a sketch done in charcoal with her turned away from the viewer. All it revealed was a portion of the right side of her face, her bare shoulder and the sweep of her hair.

Her bio was just the opposite. It was full of details—but the details were lies. The post-office box to which buyers were to send payment for her art was in New Jersey, not New York City.

"And did people buy her art?" Gulliver asked.

"Some. Mostly other art kids."

"But not all."

Shea smiled the Happy Meal smile he flashed when you got to where he wanted you to go. Gulliver had seen it before.

"One person bought most of it," Shea said. "A man named Igor Telenovich. He also wrote to her all the time. Scroll down to the bottom of the 'About Bellartgirl' page. See? There's a box for sending messages to her. At first his messages were pretty plain. Stuff about how much he loved her work and how with the right teaching she could be great. She would thank him and be nice. Then after a few months, his messages started getting weird. I have all of them printed out for you. He started asking to meet her. He offered to be her teacher. He said he could make her great. Then they turned threatening."

"Threatening?"

"You can read for yourself. But they aren't threatening like, I will kill you. He says he must save her from herself. He will take her and teach her and make her great. That it would be a crime to waste her talent, and how he can't let that happen." Shea stopped to let his words have their full impact on Gulliver.

"Go on."

"Once his messages got weird, Bella seems to have abandoned the site. This guy spooked her. She no longer responded to sales requests and didn't answer when people wrote to her."

"And you say this was two years ago?"

Shea nodded. "Look at your screen," he said, clicking his mouse.

And there on Gulliver's screen were two side-by-side photographs. Both showed an older man with gray hair and a gaunt face.

Gulliver said, "Igor Telenovich."

"That's him. The photo on the right is from Plandome Art Institute on Long Island, where he used to teach painting. The one on the left is from—"

Gulliver finished the sentence. "The closed-circuit video outside Bella's building in Brooklyn."

"That's right, Mr. Dowd. I think this Telenovich guy has her somewhere."

"The Phantom of the Opera," Gulliver said to himself.

"What?"

"Never mind. What about this guy? Where is he? You said he used to teach at the Plandome Art Institute. Why not any longer?"

"It's all printed out for you there, and I've sent all this to your computer. Telenovich was fired."

"Why?"

Shea shrugged. "It's not clear why. The when is more important."

"About two years ago," Gulliver said.

"Twenty-two months ago. It took him most of that time to track Bella down."

"How?"

Shea said, "I may be the best at this, but I'm not the only one who does it, Mr. Dowd. He might have even taught himself how to do it."

"That's not important now."

Gulliver collected all the materials Happy Meal had printed for him and turned to leave.

"You may have found Bella, Sha'wan. Maybe even saved her life. Thank you."

"You saved me, Mr. Dowd. Go get her. I like her work, and she is beautiful."

"Do you think so?"

"The most beautiful girl I have ever seen."

Gulliver smiled and left.

SEVENTEEN

Tony and Ahmed met Gulliver at his office. He filled them in on Telenovich and the possible Phantom of the Opera scenario.

"I have a source who thinks it's likely this guy has her stashed somewhere," Gulliver said.

That started a debate between them about whether to call the local cops. It lasted through most of the ride from Brooklyn, through Queens and past the Nassau County line. Gulliver pointed out, "Once the cops get involved, they're in control. It becomes their show, and they run it. We'd be watching from the sidelines."

"And we don't even know if this is where he has Bella or even if he has her for sure," Tony said.

Ahmed argued hard to call in the cops.

"There's a reason they control everything," he said. "It's 'cause they know what they're doing in these situations. Navy Seals get all kinds of training for all kinds of assaults, but this, man…We don't even know for sure what we're dealing with."

In the end, Gulliver and Tony outvoted Ahmed. And they decided they could always call the police if they felt they had to. If they got in over their heads. Gulliver laughed when Tony used that phrase. "Then we better call the cops now," he said. "I'm always getting in over my head."

They all laughed at that. The laughter didn't last long. Gulliver read aloud from the intel that Happy Meal had gathered about Telenovich.

"He's a classically trained artist. Studied in Moscow, Paris, London and New York. He was a minor success in the early eighties but has been teaching at different schools to support his art. He was at the Parker School in Boston for fifteen years. But he was dismissed in 2002. The reasons are unclear. The rumor is he became involved with one of his female students, and when she wanted to end it…you can guess the rest. The school didn't want its rep hurt, so they quietly let him go and didn't share the details with the next school he worked at. Or the next."

"Did he do bad stuff to the girl?" Tony asked, though it didn't look like he was sure he wanted to hear the answer.

"No," Gulliver said. "Nothing like that. He just became obsessed. Wouldn't leave her alone. Followed her. Like that.

"When Bella started selling her art online, Telenovich bought a lot of it," he continued. "He wrote her messages about how talented she was, but that she needed help."

Ahmed was curious. "Help?"

"His help," Gulliver answered. "He wanted to be her teacher. He said that art school would ruin her talent if that's the path she decided to take. He said he saw greatness in her, but that only he could free it. At first she liked his attention, and they wrote back and forth to each other. But then he went too far. Here, let me read this last note he sent her.

"Bellartgirl: You have no choice but to be great. And as I have said many times, only I can let that greatness out of you. Even if I must remove the skin you wear to hide it, I will do that. If I must beat it out of you or starve it out of you, I will do that. There is no escaping your greatness or me.

I don't know who you are, but I will someday. I don't know where you live, but I will. Nothing will stop me. You will be mine. Your soul. Your heart. Your art will all belong to me. I will be your maestro. Your master. Let me be that. IG.

"After that, Bella basically abandoned the website. I'm sure she was just afraid to tell her parents what she had done. And maybe she was afraid of what Joey might do. Maybe IG was harmless, and she didn't want his blood on her hands."

Tony was mad. "Stop talking bull, Dowd. What blood?"

"You wiseguys crack me up, Tony. You think it's easy growing up in your world? Bella's a smart and sensitive girl. You can hide stuff for only so long from kids. It was only a matter of time before Bella and her sisters discovered what her father did to people who got in his way. How many people have you hurt or killed for your boss, Tony?

And if Bella ever found out you were her real dad, do you think that would change anything?"

Tony opened his mouth to say something. No words came out. Even he knew it was pointless to argue. Gulliver was right. They rode the rest of the way in silence.

EIGHTEEN

The last known address for Igor Telenovich was in the incorporated village of Manorhaven. Manorhaven was the poor relation of Port Washington, an upper-middle-class area on the north shore of Long Island. And directly north of Manorhaven was the ritzy area of Sands Point. Many people believed Sands Point was the model for East Egg in F. Scott Fitzgerald's *The Great Gatsby*. But no one in Ahmed Foster's Escalade was thinking about Gatsby's mansion, his wild parties or the green light on Daisy's dock. They were thinking of Bella.

Telenovich's rented house was a drab-looking split-level ranch on a side street off Cambridge Avenue. Gulliver shook his head at the sight of it. He had seen some of Telenovich's work. He liked it. He liked it a lot. The figures in his realistic paintings seemed alive, almost as if they were breathing. As if they could walk off the canvas. Yet he lived here in such a dull house. Lifeless. Boring. It was like the cobbler whose kids went barefoot. Or the contractor whose house was the most rundown on the block.

The plan was for Gulliver to knock on the door and distract Telenovich. And if there was one thing Gulliver Dowd could do without even trying, it was to distract. His height. His misshapen body. They were enough to draw people's attention. But it was his handsome face that really did the trick. People were stunned and often speechless at the contradiction of him. It was why people pitied him so. How many times in his life had people said cruel things about the waste of such a handsome face on such a useless body? He had stopped counting. And if his appearance wasn't distracting enough, there was always his gun.

Gulliver hobbled out of the SUV and made his way toward the front door. He looked to his left and right to make sure Ahmed and Tony were in place at the sides of the house. The front of the house was dark, but there was an old VW Bug in the driveway. Old VWs had their engines in the rear. Gulliver touched the back hood. It was warm. That meant the car had been used recently, and Telenovich was likely home.

Everything was going smoothly, though it might have been better if the artist wasn't home. Gulliver wasn't against breaking into a house if it meant finding a missing kid or saving a life. That was another reason he hadn't called the cops. As he knocked, he got a weird feeling. Since he'd been at Happy Meal's house, Gulliver had been sure it was Telenovich who had Bella. But now, as he stood waiting for the artist to answer the door, Gulliver was no longer 100 percent sure. When the door pulled back, that weird feeling got even stronger.

Telenovich's eyes widened at the sight of Gulliver Dowd. "Can I help you?" the artist asked. He had a slight accent and a polite manner.

"I think so," Gulliver said. "My name is Gulliver Dowd, and I'm here about Bella."

Although Telenovich smiled, it was a sad smile. His whole body sagged. Gulliver knew defeat when he saw it.

"Please, come in, Mr. Dowd." Telenovich waved for Gulliver to enter.

They settled into a comfortable den. The walls were covered with paintings and drawings. Many of them were by Bella Vespucci. Telenovich's eyes followed Gulliver's gaze.

"Yes, Mr. Dowd. I purchased all of these from her when I knew her only as Bellartgirl. She could be great."

"I know you think that. I've read your messages to her."

Telenovich shook his head and smiled that sad smile. "What a foolish old man I am, no? I was an idiot. When she stopped writing me back to me, I realized I had driven her away. I have felt such shame since."

"You don't have her, do you?" Gulliver asked.

The artist looked shocked. "Have her! What are you talking about?"

"She's been missing for a month. That's why I'm here."

Telenovich went pale. "Oh my god. Oh my god. No. No. I would never hurt her. Those things I wrote…that was why I tracked her down. I had to apologize for driving her away. She has such promise.

You cannot understand. I am good, but I had training with some of the best. She could be so much better than I could ever be. She has such talent. The world needs the kind of beauty she can bring it. The world can be such an ugly place."

Gulliver agreed. "That note you gave her roommate at FIT. Was that—"

"My apology." He nodded. "I didn't want to frighten her, so I thought a note passed to her from her roommate would be good. Safe."

"Then why have you been hanging around her building?"

Telenovich beamed. "Because I have found a major art dealer who wants to display her work. I wanted to be the one to tell her. I know that is selfish of me— and silly. But I thought it was a good way to make a real apology. To give her something as a gesture. I thought she must forgive my stupidity with such an offer.

Aren't old men allowed their pride and foolishness?"

They talked for a few more minutes, and then Gulliver thanked Telenovich for his time. The artist begged Gulliver to tell him any news of Bella. Gulliver agreed.

Ahmed and Tony were back in the Caddy by the time Gulliver returned.

"We didn't find nothing in his basement," Tony said. "We had a clear view through four windows."

Ahmed added, "And I had a look through an attic vent. Nothing. Man, I can't be climbing up the sides of houses anymore."

"He doesn't have her," Gulliver said.

Tony didn't like hearing this. "What the hell you talking about? He has to have her."

Gulliver explained Telenovich's story. Tony didn't want to believe it, but he gave in.

"Look, Tony, if you want to come back and sit on the man's house, go ahead. But I don't think it will do you any good."

Ahmed spoke. "So we're back to square one."

"Maybe not," Gulliver said. "I've got an idea I need to check out. If I'm right, Bella is fine and safe. For now, let's all go get some sleep."

NINETEEN

It had bothered Gulliver from the beginning, but he had chosen to ignore the
voice in his head. That alone should
have gotten his attention. Every time he
ignored his instincts, he got in trouble. Or
he wound up doing twice the work to get
to the same place. By no means was the
voice in his head always right. He wasn't
a seer. He could not predict the future.
Most of the time he had trouble making
sense of the past.

Why had he ignored the voice? Because
the people involved in this case weren't

like the ones in any of his other cases. This case involved a Mafia don, his muscle-man bodyguard, the woman they both loved and a missing child. And although Gulliver had attacked the case as he would most others, he hadn't done it exactly like he had in the past. He hadn't spoken to the missing girl's mother.

The mother was often the key to finding a missing daughter. Mothers knew things about their daughters. They knew things about them they weren't even aware they knew. Little habits. Warning signs. Things that set them off. Yet, in spite of this, Gulliver hadn't asked to speak to Maria. Was it out of fear? Respect? Was it because he knew Tony and Maria's secret? It could have been any one of those reasons. Maybe it was a little bit of them all.

But while he was in Igor Telenovich's den, it had struck Gulliver. Not only hadn't he asked to speak to the mother, but the mother had not asked to speak to him. That was what had been bothering him. The mother of the missing child always asked to speak with him. Always. The mothers were usually the frantic ones no matter what the child's age. The fathers always tried to act tough and calm. The mothers were the ones who called him every day. The ones who asked the hard questions. The ones who canvassed the streets with him night and day if that's what he needed. But he hadn't heard a word from Bella's mother. And that was about to change.

They met at Hale's Bar on Smith Street in Cobble Hill, Brooklyn, which was only a mile or two from Gulliver's office. The bar wasn't open yet, but Gulliver was pals with David, the owner. David was glad to let Gulliver use an empty table now and then. He brewed a pot of coffee for Gulliver and his company. Afterward he went into the basement to do inventory.

Gulliver hadn't wanted to risk meeting on Staten Island. Too many prying eyes. Too many people who might spot Maria Vespucci. For Maria's sake and for Tony's, no one could hear what Gulliver had to say to them. He had no doubt that if Joey Vespucci ever found out how Bella had come to be, there would be blood. Tony's blood. Joey wouldn't hurt the mother of his children. But he could make Maria's life very unpleasant. Gulliver felt there was no need to risk any of that.

There was a knock at the side door. Gulliver got up and let Maria and Tony inside. He locked the door behind them. Gulliver had only seen photos of Maria. In the flesh, it was easy to see why men fell for her. In her mid-fifties, she was still classically beautiful. She had thick black hair that shone under the light. Not a hair out of place. She had high, sculpted cheekbones. Her skin was naturally dark. Except for her eyes, she wore very little makeup. Though there were some lines on her face, they only added character to her charm. Her eyes were almost as black as her hair. Her mouth was a dream, her teeth white and straight. Her lips had a lovely shape. Her legs were long. Her body curvy. And she knew just how to dress to enhance her looks. She didn't wear too much jewelry. But the jewelry she did wear was custom-made and expensive. Yet for all her beauty and class, there was an air of great sadness about her.

"Mr. Dowd," she said, offering her hand. "You have something to tell me about Bella?"

Even her voice had a smoky, sexy quality.

Gulliver shook her hand and nodded at the booth where they were to sit. "Please call me Gulliver."

"Call me Maria."

After Tony and Maria sat, Gulliver poured coffee. He gave them a moment to settle in. To sip their coffee. To relax. Gulliver sat beside Tony.

"Maria, you asked me if I had something to tell you about Bella."

"That's right."

Gulliver laughed. Maria Vespucci looked shaken. Tony looked angry, and it was clear in his tone.

"What's so funny, Dowd?"

"It's not funny, Tony. It's just that we should be asking Maria whether she has something to tell us about Bella. Not the other way around."

Maria smiled a heartbreaking smile at the little man sitting across from her.

"You are a very smart man, Gulliver," she said.

"Not smart enough. Or at least, I was a little slow on the uptake."

"Will somebody tell me what the hell is going on?" Tony demanded.

Gulliver reached into his jacket pocket and grabbed a piece of paper. He unfolded it and slid it over to Tony. Tony's face went blank at the sight of the photographic images on the sheet. They were images of Maria leaving Bella's building. In some, she carried frames. In one she had a folded easel. In another she carried two plastic garbage bags full of art supplies.

Gulliver said, "Very early this morning I paid a visit to my friend who's been doing a breakdown of the closed-circuit video we got from Bella's building. Until last night, I only had him looking at male faces. When we found out it wasn't Telenovich who had Bella, I asked my guy to go back to the video and do a new search. Now you see why we should be asking Maria about Bella?"

"Maria…how could you do that to Joey? To me? I been worried out of my mind."

She reached a long elegant hand across the table and stroked Tony's cheek.

"I couldn't do it to Joey without doing it to you too. It was the only way."

Tony took her hand and kissed it. "To do what?"

It was Gulliver who answered. "To let Bella escape."

"Escape?" Tony asked. "Escape what?"

"This life, Tony," Maria said, tears rolling down her cheeks. "Bella isn't like her sisters. You know that. The other girls, they fit in. They enjoy being Joey's little girls. But Bella was never cut out to be a mob princess. This world isn't her world. The danger. The violence. The ugliness of what this life is all about. Toni and Krystal can ignore where their money comes from. Not Bella. This life would kill her. It was killing her. And I couldn't have that. Bella has a gift, and I wouldn't see that crushed."

Gulliver smiled. "It was you who wanted her to go to FIT and to have a separate apartment. Smart. It created confusion.

It gave you more time. You arranged for her to go missing."

Tony asked, "Where did she go?"

"First she was in California," Maria answered.

Tony blinked. "What do you mean?"

Gulliver said, "She means Bella's not there anymore. She's gone. Maria doesn't know where. That's the idea, Tony. It's like witness protection. If Maria doesn't know where Bella is, it's that much harder to find her. You can't tell what you don't know."

Tony looked like he might explode.

Gulliver looked directly into Maria's eyes. "This is an amazing sacrifice you've made."

"What's he talking about, Maria?" Tony asked.

"To give Bella the life she deserves, Maria has let Bella go. She might never see her again. Hard for a mother to do that, Tony. Very hard. You had an offshore numbered bank account set up for her, Maria?"

Maria nodded. "I don't know the number, so I can't be used to trace her."

Tony shook his head. "None of this shit matters. He'll find her. You don't know Joey like I know Joey. Not even you know him like I do, Maria. He'll find her."

A voice came from the hallway leading to the back room. "That's right, Tony. I'll find her."

And out of the shadows stepped the man himself, Joey Vespucci. Flanking him were two of his guys. Gulliver had seen them before. Both were younger and bigger than Tony. And Gulliver didn't doubt that either one would love to replace Tony as Joey's right hand. All three men approached the booth where Gulliver, Maria and Tony sat.

"You are the best," Vespucci said to Gulliver. "You didn't find Bella. Not exactly. But this is close enough. I'll take it from here, little man. You should leave now, or go downstairs and stay with your pal. But whatever you do, get out of this room. And don't worry—I won't lay a hand on my wife. Even if she is just a beautiful whore who slept with my best friend, she's still the mother of my girls."

Tony opened his mouth to speak. Joey didn't let him.

"Don't bother to deny it, Tony. I know the two of you had a thing back in the day. And I know it didn't last long. Everybody has their slip-ups. But now, if I don't do something about it I'll look weak. And a man like me can't afford to look weak. You know that. I'll see to you. Then I'll find my daughter, and that will be that."

Gulliver sensed Tony wasn't just going to sit there and take it. He was right.

"She's not your daughter!" Tony shouted.

Maria gasped. Vespucci's eyes got big. It was clear he'd known about the affair but not about Bella. His face twisted into an ugly red mask. He had promised he wouldn't touch Maria, but this news was obviously too much for him to take. He slapped his wife across the face, splitting her lip.

"Whore!" he screamed at her. "How could you have lived with me and slept in my bed all these years and kept this from me? Whore!"

He raised his hand to slap her again.

But before Vespucci could bring his hand down on his wife's face a second time, Tony pulled his piece. He shot his boss through the hand that had slapped Maria.

"You disloyal son of a bitch!" Vespucci raged. "I'm going to—"

He didn't finish the sentence, because Tony shot his boss and best friend through the heart. Vespucci didn't fall. Not for a few seconds. And in those stunned seconds before Joey fell to the bar floor, Gulliver dove over the table and knocked Maria to the floor. He threw himself over her. Just as he landed atop her, Joey's lifeless body collapsed. His head made a sickening thud against the tiles.

Without instructions from their boss, Vespucci's bodyguards hesitated, and that proved to be a fatal mistake. Above Maria and Gulliver, the din and smoke of gunfire filled the air. Another body dropped. Then another. The noise stopped as suddenly as it had started. Maria tried to get up, but Gulliver held her down. Then, finally, a fourth body hit the floor. Tony's.

Gulliver crawled off Maria. He took out his weapon and checked Vespucci and his men. Maria checked Tony. Joey Vespucci was dead. He was probably dead before he hit the floor. One of his men was also dead. The other was still alive—barely. Gulliver kicked that man's gun away and called 9-1-1. After that he turned to Tony.

Maria was crying. She had Tony's head cradled in her lap. She was pressing her hand down on a red hole in the middle of his chest. There was blood all over her clothes and her hands. Gulliver could see that Tony was already in shock and wouldn't live for more than another minute. If that.

"That was a brave thing you did, Tony."

Tony smiled. He coughed up blood. Then he said, "Listen, Bug...I don't know why he did it...but the guy who killed... your sis—" Tony stopped speaking, his whole body clenching as if it were one big fist. Then he relaxed a bit. "He's dead."

Gulliver clutched Tony's shoulders. "How do you know that?"

"I put two pills...in his ear. Joey had me do it last year...after your cop friend was murdered. Joey said...he owed you that much."

Then Tony's body clenched again. And this time when it relaxed, it relaxed forever.

Maria looked more shocked than any-thing else. Then she said, "I don't know how to get in touch with Bella."

Gulliver stood, placed his hand on her shoulder and said, "Don't worry. News like this spreads. She'll read about it."

"I loved them both."

"I know."

Gulliver tried to think of something else to say. But there was nothing to say in the face of so much blood and devotion.

TWENTY

Gulliver didn't have his answers. He had an answer. He didn't know why Keisha had been killed, and now he probably never would. Did he take some satisfaction in knowing her killer had also been killed? Some, he guessed. But the important thing was, he had come to as if out of a long coma. Keisha was dead, and nothing would bring her back. Knowing why she'd been killed was no longer as important to him as it had once been, he realized. Living was what was important. Loving was what was important. Perhaps more important than anything in the universe. What else mattered without love?

And so, armed with that thought, Gulliver stood in front of the door to the condo he had bought for Mia. He raised his right hand and knocked. He waited. And as he did, he looked down at the blue-velvet-covered ring case in his left hand. As he waited, he hoped Mia liked diamonds and emeralds. He hoped she remembered how to say yes.

ACKNOWLEDGMENTS

Thanks to Bob Tyrrell for taking a chance on Gulliver. Also to David Hale Smith and Erin Mitchell. To my friend and super Gulliver fan Marjorie Tucker.

But none of this would be worth it without the love and support of Rosanne, Kaitlin and Dylan. Thanks guys.

Called a "hard-boiled poet" by National Public Radio's Maureen Corrigan and the "noir poet laureate" in the *Huffington Post,* REED FARREL COLEMAN is the author of twenty-one novels and novellas. He has been signed to do the next four books in Robert B. Parker's Jesse Stone series and by Putnam to begin a new series of his own. He is a three-time recipient of the Shamus Award and a three-time Edgar Award nominee in three different categories. He has also won the Audie, Macavity, Barry, and Anthony awards. He lives with his family on Long Island. For more information, visit www.reedcoleman.com.

Discover the first three titles in the Gulliver Dowd mystery series

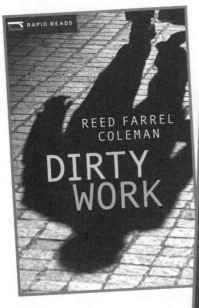

RAPID READS

REED FARREL COLEMAN

DIRTY WORK

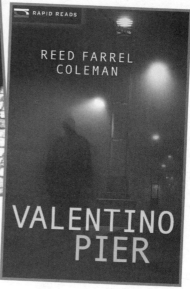

RAPID READS

REED FARREL COLEMAN

VALENTINO PIER